THE ADVENTURE FRIENDS

Lost Dog

D0103569

Read more books in
THE ADVENTURE FRIENDS series!

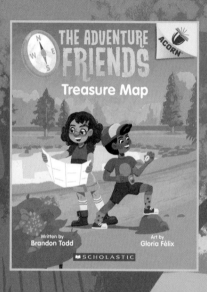

THE ADVENTURE FRIENDS
ACORN

Treasure Map

Written by
Brandon Todd

Art by
Gloria Félix

SCHOLASTIC

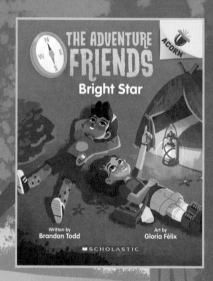

THE ADVENTURE FRIENDS
ACORN

Bright Star

Written by
Brandon Todd

Art by
Gloria Félix

SCHOLASTIC

THE ADVENTURE FRIENDS

Lost Dog

WRITTEN BY
Brandon Todd

ART BY
Gloria Félix

ACORN™
SCHOLASTIC INC.

For Mom and Dad, who encouraged
my exploration and imagination.
—BT

To Kumo, Nube, Mochi,
and the future friends we'll make.
—GF

Text copyright © 2023 by Brandon Todd
Illustrations copyright © 2023 by Gloria Félix

Library of Congress Cataloging-in-Publication Data

Names: Todd, Brandon, author. | Félix, Gloria, illustrator.
Title: Lost dog / written by Brandon Todd; illustrated by Gloria Félix.
Description: New York : Scholastic, Inc., [2023] | Series: The adventure
friends ; 2 | Audience: Ages 5–7. | Audience: Grades K–2. | Summary:
"Miguel and Clarke help a neighbor find their lost dog, Spider. They
grab their walking sticks and map. Then they set out to search the
woods. Across four short stories, their adventure leads them to Spider
—and to the perfect spot for a secret fort!"—Provided by publisher.
Identifiers: LCCN 2022003902 (print) |
ISBN 9781338805857 (paperback) | ISBN 9781338805864 (library binding)
Subjects: CYAC: Dogs—Fiction. | Lost and found possessions—Fiction. |
Maps—Fiction. | Friendship—Fiction. | LCGFT: Picture books.
Classification: LCC PZ7.1.T6125 Lo 2023 (print) | DDC [E]—dc23
LC record available at https://lccn.loc.gov/2022003902

10 9 8 7 6 5 4 3 2 1   23 24 25 26 27

Printed in China   62
First printing, May 2023
Edited by Katie Carella
Art Direction by Brian LaRossa
Book design by Jaime Lucero

RO465599301

TABLE OF CONTENTS

MEET THE CHARACTERS

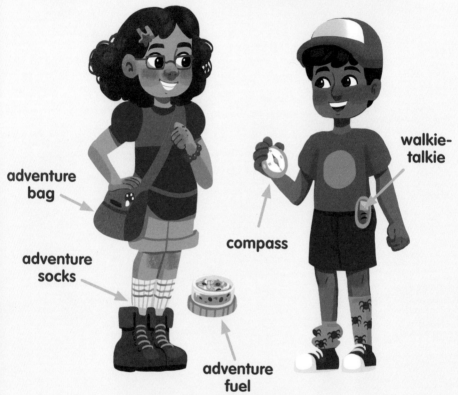

adventure bag

walkie-talkie

adventure socks

compass

adventure fuel
(This is what Clarke calls her mom's trail mix!)

Clarke
Code Name:
Thunder Walrus
New to town.
Loves planning, drawing,
and ADVENTURE!

Miguel
Code Name:
Captain Compass
Knows everyone in town.
Loves bugs, surprises,
and ADVENTURE!

MISSING SPIDER

Clarke was new to town.
There were lots of new things in her life.

She had a new house, a new room, and a new walkie-talkie.

She also had a new friend named Miguel. They were **adventure friends**.

Clarke's walkie-talkie buzzed.

"Come in, Thunder Walrus. This is Captain Compass. Do you copy?" said Miguel. "That's walkie-talkie for 'Can you hear me?'"

Clarke was ready for adventure.

She grabbed the **adventure map**.

She put on her **adventure socks**.

And she headed out.

Clarke picked up her walkie-talkie.
"I hear you loud and clear," she said.

"Let's go on an adventure!" said Mi

"I will be right over," said Clarke.

Miguel was talking to a neighbor.

"Hi, Clarke! This is Rita," said Miguel.
"She is our mayor. She is the boss
of the whole town!"

"Wow," said Clarke. "That's really cool!"

"I hear you're making a map of our town," said Rita.

"Yes," said Clarke. "Do you want to see it?"

Clarke showed Rita their **adventure map**.

"Wow," said Rita. "That's cool too!"

"You two really know your way around," said Rita. "I could use your help. My Spider has run off again."

"You have a pet spider?" asked Clarke.

Miguel laughed. "Spider is Rita's dog," he said.

Clarke laughed too.

Rita showed Clarke a photo of Spider.

"As mayor, I work at City Hall," said Rita. "Spider loves to play in the woods behind the building."

That gave Miguel an idea.

"We should look for him in the woods," said Miguel.

"Will he follow us when we find him?"
asked Clarke.

"Spider loves treats," said Rita.
"Give him these and say, 'Vamos!'
Then he won't leave your side."

"What does 'Vamos!' mean?"
asked Clarke.

"It means 'Let's go!'" said Miguel.

"You can count on us," Clarke told Rita.

She put the dog treats in her bag,
right next to her **adventure fuel**.

"Vamos!" shouted Clarke and Miguel.

THE HIKE

Clarke and Miguel stood under
a street sign.

"Today's mission is to find Spider,"
said Clarke.

"I am ready!" said Miguel.

Clarke and Miguel looked at the map.
Rita said the woods were
behind City Hall.

Miguel pointed to the map.
"This is where City Hall should be,"
he said.

Then Miguel took out his compass.

He lined up the red needle with the **N**.
That's how to find **NORTH, SOUTH,
EAST,** or **WEST** on a compass.

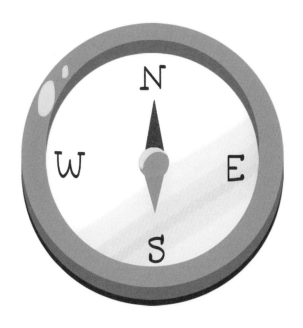

"We need to go **NORTH**," said Clarke.

They walked **NORTH** past some houses.
They reached the edge of the map.
They found City Hall!

Clarke added it to the map.

"I see the woods," said Clarke. "Let's go!"

"Wait," said Miguel. He was looking at the ground.

"What are you looking for?" asked Clarke.

"Walking sticks," said Miguel, "so we don't trip and fall." He picked up two very large sticks.

"Good idea," said Clarke.

They hiked into the woods.

They passed under a tunnel of trees.

They saw a creek filled with frogs.

They crossed an old wooden bridge.

Clarke added each landmark to the map.

"Landmarks show us where we've been," she said. "These are our street signs in the woods."

"Good idea," said Miguel.

"We found a lot on our hike," said Miguel. "But we haven't found Spider."

"I need a break," said Clarke.
"Let's have a snack."

Clarke and Miguel sat down
on a fallen tree.

Miguel grabbed a handful of
adventure fuel from Clarke's bag.

"YUCK!" said Miguel. He dropped the
rest to the ground.

"OOPS!" said Clarke. "That wasn't
adventure fuel. Those were Spider's
dog treats!"

Just then, they heard a noise
in the bushes.

"Something is coming," said Clarke.

"Spider!" said Miguel.

Spider ate the treats that Miguel
had dropped on the fallen tree.

Then Spider jumped down below.

"Where did he go?" asked Clarke.

She looked under the fallen tree.
There was a secret room.

Spider sat by a pile of balls. There were
baseballs, tennis balls, and golf balls.

Spider wagged his tail.

"This is where he keeps his toys!"
said Clarke. "That's why he keeps
running off."

Miguel smiled.
"I'm glad we found Spider," he said.
"Rita will be glad too!"

SECRET FORT

Clarke and Miguel sat with Spider.
They gave him treats.

Miguel looked around.
"This secret room would be a cool fort,"
he said.

Clarke looked around.
"Yes! It just needs a little work,"
she said.

Clarke and Miguel got to work.

Clarke dragged in a log for a bench.

Miguel hung up his compass.

Together, they found a flat rock for a table.

Even Spider organized his toys.

Now it was a very cool fort.

"Let's test our walkie-talkies," said Clarke. "I want to see how far they go."

Miguel grabbed his compass and the map. "I'll call you at each landmark," he said.

Miguel walked **WEST**.

He reached the old bridge.
"Thunder Walrus, do you copy?"
asked Miguel over the walkie-talkie.

"I hear you loud and clear," said Clarke.

Miguel walked down to the creek.
"Do you copy?" asked Miguel.

"Yes!" said Clarke.

Miguel made it to the tunnel of trees.
"Do you copy?" asked Miguel.

Clarke didn't answer.

It was time to turn back.

On his way back, Miguel called Clarke. "Do you copy?" he asked.

Miguel held his walkie-talkie to his ear.

"I hear you, Captain Compass," said Clarke. "And now I see you too!"

Clarke and Miguel sat on the log.
Spider sat by his toys.

"Our fort needs a top-secret name,"
said Miguel.

"The Secret Fort?" asked Clarke.

"That is a good name," said Miguel.
"But it's not very secret."

Clarke looked around. Spider's toys looked like bird's eggs.

"How about the Spider's Nest?" said Clarke.

"That's perfect!" said Miguel.

"Arf!" said Spider. He thought it was perfect too.

SPIDER'S TREATS

Miguel, Clarke, and Spider sat in their fort.

"Let's take Spider back to Rita," said Clarke.

"Do you think he will follow us?"
asked Miguel.

Clarke looked in her **adventure bag**.
"I hope so," she said. "But we're almost
out of dog treats."

Miguel said,
"Vamos!"

Clarke gave
Spider treats.

Spider stayed by their side.

They passed the old wooden bridge,
the creek filled with frogs, and the tunnel
of trees. They knew right where to go.

Soon, they were at City Hall.

Clarke reached for a treat.
"OH NO!" she said.

"We are out of treats!" said Clarke.

"I know where we can get more!"
said Miguel.

Miguel walked SOUTH.
He stopped at Sweet Al's Bakery.

Clarke added the bakery to her map.

MAIN ST

5th

4th

2ND

3RD

TRAIL ST

1 st

OAK

PARK

"Al has tons of treats," said Miguel.
"I bet he has something for Spider."

Clarke smelled the freshly baked goods.
"Let's find something for us too," she said.

Miguel talked to Al. He told him about their adventure.

"Do you sell dog treats?" Clarke asked.

Al pointed to two special jars.

Spider wagged his tail.

Al gave them two cookies and
one dog treat.

Miguel asked for his own bag. He didn't
want to eat another dog treat.

Clarke gave Spider the special dog treat.
He stayed by their side all the way
to Rita's house.

Rita was very happy to see Spider.

Spider was very happy to see Rita.

Clarke and Miguel were happy
to eat their cookies.

"Thank you," said Rita. "I can tell Spider
likes you both."

Miguel looked at Spider. "Do you want to be an **adventure friend** too?" he asked.

Spider barked.

"Welcome to the **adventure friends**!" said Clarke.

About the Creators

Brandon Todd lives in North Kansas City, Missouri. When he was a kid, he made treasure maps of the woods by his house. The biggest treasure he found was three golf balls! He is the author and illustrator of a picture book called TOU-CAN'T!: A LITTLE SISTER STORY. The Adventure Friends is his first early reader series.

Gloria Félix was born and raised in Uruapan, a city in Michoacán, Mexico. This beautiful, small city is one of her biggest inspirations when it comes to her art. In addition to children's books, Gloria makes art for the animation industry. Her hobbies include walking, life drawing, and plein-air painting with her friends. Currently, she lives and paints in Guadalajara.

YOU CAN DRAW MIGUEL!

1 Draw the outline of Miguel's head, shirt, and shorts.

2 Draw the outline of his hair, arms, and legs. Give him a hat!

3 Draw a circle in his hand. That's the compass. Add details to his hands, shorts, and shoes.

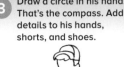

4 Draw Miguel's face and ear. Add a walkie-talkie on his hip.

5 Add details to Miguel's shirt and socks. Don't forget to add a needle on the compass!

6 Color in your drawing!

WHAT'S YOUR STORY?

Clarke and Miguel make a fort in the woods.
Imagine **you** have a secret fort. Where would it be?
What landmarks would lead to your fort?
How would you make it cool?
Write and draw your story!